light
needs darkness to
shine

mehran hashemi
aka: hush m e

for all the bright souls who believe in the power of
their lights and appreciate darkness

contents

sunrise

the green breath

we met before

in dreams

let's date

in

reality

you're so far away

yet i don't feel the distance

because once you said

we're under

the same sky

you smiled

and i got goosebumps

because i knew

i fell in love

moon caught the sun's attention

with the beauty of her reflection

among those shining stars

her scars meant to be

perfection

she was crying

and i gave her my handkerchief

her makeup made the tears into ink

and she shed

the beautiful poetry

light needs darkness to shine

i wrote for the moon

on the snow

then it melted away

by the

jealous sun

for feeling the gravity

i denied the falling apple

as i felt my heart

falling for you

t h r e e words kissed my ears

and found a way into my brain

i blocked my heart not to hear

but it was already *in my veins*

i found a jasmine

in your heart

it smelled home

though we were apart

i couldn't live there for a lifetime

yet your scent remained

in my art

people read my poems

and ask how she looks

and i say even the poetry

can't describe in thousand books

when you smiled

        your eyes glittered

my heart flipped

        and love flickered

your blue eyes were meant to be a prompt to inspire

me with an *ocean of thoughts*

i wanted to be an ordinary writer

so i wrote simply something about you

but you made me so famous

for discovering

a new star

if you are into music

come closer and hug me

let our hearts meet

to play a drumbeat

once upon a time

we used to write for each other

in the nights

on the sky

when the moon

was our *connection*

/

the chemical reaction

made by our eye contacts

was a *new formula*

not written in any books

but discovered by our hearts

i read my poem

then i saw your gaze

so i recited more

from your eyes

it was a beautiful war

when we met

you couldn't resist

looking at me

and i was fighting

to tame my heart

the eyes of a woman

may seem like shallow pools

that's why you dare to jump

but when you do

you wish there were a rescue team
in the middle of the ocean

the way you look at me

is a crime

as you shoot me

with the bullets of your eyes

and i fall for you

and hit the ground

i could never imagine

the moon would reach the sun

until i saw you

holding
the sunflower

if the rainbow had a taste

it would be as luscious as

the lollipop's sweetness

that remained

on your lips

you and i

when we hear

our favorite song

and look at each other

our eyes don't look

same as always

and only you and i

know the difference

light needs darkness to shine

the only *whirlpools*

i'd love to drown in

and never survive

are your eyes

your eyes

were like lie detectors

when they stared at mine

my heart revealed the secret

that my lips never dared to say

your smile is the sunshine

that my soul is absorbing

and when my eyes rain

it gives my heart a

rainbow

to become an astronomer

they need the sky

i need your eyes

suddenly

her name healed

her broken heart

by being kissed

between his lips

i love me

when i'm with you

you make me feel

special

like a man

who finds a

diamond

i saw your *dimple*

when you smiled

it was a pure beauty

of a blessed blossom

i used to take pictures

of the sky

then i saw her

a girl whose hair was painted

with the golden brush of the sun

a glowing frecklefaced

more beautiful than the moon

and those pretty blue eyes

were like undiscovered galaxies

and i got so happy

because i found

the whole universe

simply in her

light needs darkness to shine

sunshine

the hungry flames

hush me

with a wild kiss

as if you want to sew my lips

then my heart will talk to you

by every single one it beats

the locked-up piano desires a warm touch from the

pianist to get rid of her soul's dust and moan for him

a seductive piece

light needs darkness to shine

i achieved *vision*

when i closed my eyes

and opened my heart

to taste more of your lips

between her legs

i found a pink blossom

it was already wet

before i wanted to water

i went deep through you

like i was the wave

and you were the seashore

where i wanted to exceed

and proceed to your land

with the torrent of my ink

since she heard his heartbeat

her soul couldn't stop dancing

since he saw the way she moves

his heart couldn't stop

clapping

the lovers closed their eyes to kiss

it made me close mine too

they did to taste love

i did

to touch you in *poetry*

the untouched naked flower

desires a kiss from the breeze

to spread her seductive fragrance

for being touched by the bees

your lips rubbed mine

and my *dangerous tongue*

struck the match

to set fire to your heart

open your thirsty mouth

suck my soul's release

with your hungry lips

swallow the juicy words

let them swim to your mind

and make your musings wet

to soak your sinful thoughts

and water your blooming fantasy

i will drown you in an ocean of desires

and you will sink with me

in my dripping luscious ink

i smelled your pink petals

and inhaled their fragrance

it made me lose my mind

and become *addicted* to you

i'm a man

reckless enough

not to see the borders

nor to understand

what boundaries are

so i cross the line

even the other side is a hell

i walk on the mines

and burn into flames

of a forbidden love

there is a garden

inside of you

where i'd love to

plant my seeds

to have more flowers

like you

nature takes my strength

and in return

she gives me peace

and this is how we make love

i'd love to make you wet

and smell your scent

a kind of fragrance

that even fresh flowers

would wish to spread

on a rainy day

beg me for more drops

of the drug in my ink

so i inject your heart

slowly with my quill

to come into your blood

and make you feel me within

deep into your heart

and deep into your thoughts

then you'll go high and laugh

for being addicted to me

we closed our eyes

to open our hearts

and what they saw

was luscious enough

to satisfy

our hunger

i flirt with you

in my dreams

and burn in the flames

        of a *secret desire*

i dip the tip of my tongue into your honeypot

you bit your pink lips grabbing my head

and pushing me ahead to lick between your legs

a luscious taste of heaven made me lose my mind

and find myself in somewhere else

in a garden of flowers

like a bee, i craved to suck

and touch your wet petals to make you squirt

the sweetest liquid

i desire to play

with your hair

to hear your heart

moaning the *lustful notes*

the calmness of the night

doesn't get how i feel

and how my heart beats

when i kiss your lips

i want to make love with your mind

i want to release my words inside your thoughts

to hear you moaning that it feels so hot

to hear you screaming that it hits you hard

to make your eyes wet

when my words come

sunset

the crying shadows

mehran hashemi

you leave me

while i live you

my darkest nightmares

are the hazy memories

that were one day

my brightest dreams

you could stop loving me

while i couldn't stop playing

our *favorite song*

on the cold days ahead

thousand cups of coffee

wouldn't help me

to get warm

as your smile could

she's lost

in the joy of love

trying to fly above

to where the eagle flies

yet she's just
a dove

my soul is captured

by a *photographer*

who takes shots

of the old memories

and turns them into poetry

i knew that i'm going to lose you

as i saw the rainbow

the sunset and the snow

as today's beauty fades tomorrow

the ice-cold crystal tears hailing from her frozen

heart the snowfalls of her eyes are building a

diamond castle

the yellow leaf commits suicide

to feel how it is to be free

she couldn't stand their green side

she no longer belonged to the tree

a dim memory sparkled in her mind

kindled and set fire to her soul

the thoughts turned into flames

her dreams burned in the blaze

the broken hearted wanderer

is following her footprints

and trying to smell

the *faded memories*

a glass broke into pieces

        and i tried to pick them up

but they hurt my hands

        to tell me how *it hurts*

you didn't want me

i know

and i don't want you anymore

but if i could travel in time

i'd love you again

i'm sure

i woke up

when i needed you

to linger more in my dreams

now i'm sober and craving *a single shot*

of memories

in the roads of my thoughts

i see a shadow

a wanderer who seems to be a stranger

yet my heart knows

the passenger

i show your picture

to the people around

and ask where you are

they point at my heart

my inner child blew a *dandelion*

hoping the wishes come true

the seeds got floated in the air

and buried

in the grave of hopes

you left your home in my heart

now i'm trying to sell the place

but all the visitors have said

a ghost lives in the *haunted house*

after i had to quit you

i begged everyone

to inject me with the same drug

of your love

i'm smoking a rolled letter

with lots of secrets inside

the words are smoldering

my chest is burning

he got stuck in a dark cave

so he wrote for the birds

they cried reading this message

let the man not forget the rainbow

i stared at the sun

and went blind

for looking at something

which is not mine

i chalked my dead heart's outline

waiting for you to come back

as the *criminal* always returns

to the scene of the crime

i wish i were like the birds

not because they can fly

but because they always find

the right place

to build their

home

in the solitary confinement

he's trying to count

all the lights he could have seen

in a beautiful colorful night

why would i live in reality

when the people in my dreams

know how to love me better

despite being an *introvert*

for the first time

i was looking for pain

in my frostbitten soul

to arouse my numb thoughts

kiss me on the cheek

may the love in your warm lips

melt my frozen tears

sad songs

can make a soul dance

who misses remembering

the lost memories

lost in a dark alley

in a familiar melancholy

the flickering light

is dying

a shadow is crying

she peels her skin

to unfold the layers

of her shades

to reveal the pages

of an *untold story*

the dark side of him looks like a silhouette

it's a place where his beloveds have left their

shadows

whenever i breathe deeply

i inhale the air

and the clouds too

and then

i *rain*

i denied who i am

by pretending to be

the one she loves

but i hadn't known

one day comes

that i'd sit alone

and miss both

i'm feeling like a star

happy for shining

sad for being far away

from the moon

people come and go

          like the perfumes

good ones linger more

but no one will stay

my lonely night

is void of stars

and i'm worried

about tomorrow

what if i lose the sun too

i'm fighting in silence

to silence the screams

to make peace with the things

which were one day my dreams

sometimes

you open the cage

for a bird

but she doesn't leave

not because she loves you

but because you have ruined

all the dreams where

she *wished to fly*

she's supposed to plant seeds

in a land full of mines

but how can she give birth

to the flowers

when she's already afraid of

being killed

my heart is caged

yet she dances

to the beats

she hits herself

and bleeds

for this

bloody dance

i breathe

a brooding melancholy is

when your body

is haunted

yet your soul runs

to find a way to escape

life is too short

but not for everyone

for a soul who's in pain

every second is a

lifetime

i've heard *freedom* is beautiful

yet i've never tasted it

i don't know how it feels

it's hard for me to understand

like a child

who was born blind

is taught that

beautiful colors exist

when the chest of a writer burns

her words burst into flames

that ignite papers

to break your silence

to hear you cough

as her heart is smoldering

an abandoned piece of wood

misses the color of her past

when she was tangled with hope

yet you won't see her sorrow

as she tries to hide her wounds

but those termites in her mind

are devouring her green soul

she craves to get burned

and be free of her

corrupted corpse

the snowman is staring at the window and waiting

to see her for the last time before the sunrise

i thought we were happy to play hide and seek

but i opened my eyes

and found you nowhere

i haven't talked to my heart

since you have gone

how can i convince it

that you were not the one

i get high when i overthink then i fall into ink

the shallow sounds deep as its swamp wants me to

sink

i became *homeless* right at that moment

that i found out

i can't live in your heart

i was told that jewels are at the bottom of the oceans

so i dived to go deep through but i sank into depths

of thoughts

i'm stuck in a desert looking for a drop of a miracle

i see a sea at the end of the path

but what if it's just a *mirage*

where i live

my body is ever bathed in sunshine

yet my soul always feels
            a gloomy sunday

my chest is heavy because i feel blue

and i feel the color that how it turns my blood into

dark purple

i feel the poison in all my veins

and whenever my heart sheds tears

my skin gets inked

from the very beginning

you were obsessed with the king

thinking it's your lucky card

yet you didn't notice

my ace of hearts

my little bird

you used to peck me

and i thought it was a sign of love

but since i set you free

you haven't come back to me

i'm sick of the

iced memories

even the snow

burns my heart

i'm feeling alone

among the crowd

chasing your shadow

through the darkness

nightmares chase me at night

and i chase dreams in daylight

i'm tired of this run

and i hope one of them

catches the other one

the paper is looking at me

and reading my mind

she knows how much

my heart is broken these days

yet she says

please stop

you're hurting me

i've already had enough

poetry is a magnet

to attract

all the broken hearts

moonlight

the uprising lights

mehran hashemi

don't let the darkness

    overcome your kindness

when nobody was there

to listen to me

i noticed the ears of a paper

silently wanted to hear

so i talked

then the world listened

her soul is full of scars

yet she turns them into stars

so you see a galaxy in her

meanwhile there are

the star wars

he's a writer who pushes out the words

from his heart

the pain makes him shout

while giving *birth*

to his art

don't make a decision

when you are too happy

or too sad

when you are too disappointed

or too proud

i catch the deep words

by the hook of my mind

from the bottom of my heart

to feed my *hungry soul*

you must run so hard in your life

but in the end

at the finish line

you'll take all your clothes off

to rest and celebrate in a naked soul

i learned *love*

from a tree

who's cut and killed

yet when i write

on her skin

she wants me to breathe

kill me

or don't hurt me at all

because i'm a writer

and i'm made of flesh and ink

if i bleed

you will get *stained*

the birds sing

and ask you for a dance

you accept it

then your soul flies

and joins them on the tree

for singing and asking

another soul for a dance

she kisses her scars

and loves each one

like they're her *medals*

to prove how strong she was

a sun was beating in her chest

and when people broke her heart

she started bleeding the lights

through the cracks of her soul

people might have

a colorful sky above

but i'm proud of myself

for holding my head high

to seek the *sliver lining*

through the gray shades

of the darkest clouds

if one day all my scars

faded away

i would lose my way

because those marks

    have made a map

        which i can find home with

she never wears makeup

to make up for her *imperfection*

because those flaws

have made her different

from the stars

your eyes can't see anything

either in total darkness

or in absolute brightness

and your soul needs both

not to get blind

among the silent crowd

                i heard a shout

but i was the only one

                who could hear it

as they were already deaf

                by being used to the sound

if you try to step forward

through the darkness

then you won't need

your eyes in daylight

to find

your way

the dark holes of the eyes

hug the flow of light

to make us genuinely see

yet most of us are still blind

i used to beg god for help

as i thought he was the only one

who could show me the way

but i didn't hear anything from him

this time i decided to believe in myself instead

and i realized

the god whom i was looking for

was myself

she is simply herself

in a world whose people

love to be actors

and that's why she's loved more

by the fans

for her *natural role*

ever since i realized

the world within me

is bigger than anything

the whole universe begs

my eyes to be seen

three

two

one
action

this is you on the stage

this is your time to play

follow the soundtrack

dance and dance
and dance

in the darkest time

of her life

the stars taught her

if she wants to   *shine*

she has to embrace

        the darkness

light needs darkness to shine

Amazon is not available in my country
and I didn't have access to have an account, so I
never thought that one day it would be possible for
me to be published!!
I did it with the help of a very beautiful soul and
poetess from Canada.
I want to use this last page of my book to mention
her name and thank her wholeheartedly!!

You made my wish come true!
Thank you Isabelle
AKA "beware of calm waters"

Made in the USA
Las Vegas, NV
30 December 2023

83716126R00085